THE ECLIPSE OF THALASYX

PAUL MICHAEL PETERS

COPYRIGHT

PROLOGUE

The Celestial Spider seized mid-pilgrimage, ensnared in the vast strands of the Cosmic Web. The Clavis Torqueo Monks of Gearturn jolted awake as three unbelted rule-breakers slid helplessly across the floor. Abbé disliked interruptions—even celestial ones. He and Faria, senior deacons, steadied the men and made way, offering any assistance to Captain Sheldrake.

"She just stopped—won't crawl another step on this web," Sheldrake said, staring too long through the glass. "Been with her for years. She's never refused."

From this distance, the three could see something metallic, blinking red.

"We get debris caught in the webbing regularly. Not sure why this would spook her. She's a good spider—a grand girl. Been with her for years. Must be something. Something spooked her." Captain Sheldrake shook his head. "Don't understand it."

"Have you any mobility units?" Faria asked.

"Yes, yes. Required to have one for each passenger," the captain explained. "More than your group of twelve."

"You have a plan, Faria?" Abbé asked.

"Abbé, you and I will suit up and walk the web to the object. If possible, we will extract it for safe passage."

"Yes, yes. Let's suit you two up." Sheldrake hurried them out of his watch.

The three went to the evacuation room and found two mobility units. The captain checked each with care to ensure safety and fortitude for a web walk. It took the better part of an hour, but soon, both monks were ready and at the door.

"Now, she's a bit ticklish under the legs, so mind where you step," the captain instructed. "Once she sees you get close, she's likely to help you down."

In the pressure room, the atmosphere exchange made it safe for the two to exit through the outer door. Stepping onto the white Celestial Spider's cephalothorax felt uncertain, like walking on dry sand. The crystal granules of spider skin were unexpected, deceptive from their distant appearance. As the monks approached the patella, a shimmy ran through the entire body, and the ship attached to the abdomen quaked.

"I guess she is ticklish," Abbé said, regaining balance.

When she realized that the two bodies in space suits were attempting to walk the web, she lowered her left front leg, forming a ramp for the two to traverse. With relative ease, aided by her assistance, they bounded onto the Cosmic Web with a twang.

"I've never been this close before. You?" Abbé asked.

"The Cosmic Web?" Faria replied. "Only through the portholes, passing by."

"Look at it—it must be six men wide." The communication in the helmet clicked. "Easy to walk."

"Looks safe enough." Faria inched forward.

Close behind, Abbé talked to distract himself from the looming heights and darkness. "Gearturn is innovating so fast these days, I bet they'll start to build machines that travel the Cosmic Web one day."

"Replace the Celestial Spider fleet? Never." Static followed Faria's voice.

"They could make mech—faster, last lon_"

"There are clusters of Spiders at each—" Abbé's voice got lost in the crackle. "What would they all do?"

"I'm not sure," the shorter monk replied. "But I'm sure that technology might—independent travel."

Static became more frequent in the communications as Faria said, "The Celestial Spiders build the Cosmic Web. What would—"

"What's that? I only caught part of that." Abbé called back.

"I said, the Cosmic Web is spun by Spiders," but the recurring static drowned him out.

Distant and soft at first, it began to grow louder. It seemed to coincide with each blink of the beacon's red light. As they drew closer, the static worsened—constant now.

Faria took Abbé by the arm after spotting the object. He led them back halfway, until the static grew less disruptive. In broken sentences, Abbé understood the plan that Faria communicated: "Orb. Flashes... static disruption is causing the problem. Must be electromagnetic waves—"

Faria pointed to Abbé's chest. "—and I can lift it. Bring back... inspect it there."

Abbé nodded, the fixed helmet making his whole torso dip up and down.

Returning to the device, the two men stood over it to inspect the impact. It had struck just the right spot. Abbé moved to the far side. Faria turned so he wouldn't have to walk backwards. Both bent at the knee and lifted the object. With little to no gravity, it was only a matter of guiding its direction, while the cleats on their mobility suits allowed for an awkward walk.

With each step closer, Abbé and Faria watched the spider's legs retract—pulling back and shaking from what seemed like fear, not ticklishness. Faria looked back and shrugged. With nothing but static in their ears, the two were left with hand signals and exaggerated gestures.

They set down the device, pulsing with red light. Faria waved his arms high and wide, getting the attention of Captain Sheldrake.

He spotted them and started to coax his spider companion with kind words. "Come on, girl. Help me here, darling." He pulled levers and knobs, sweet-talking her toward calm.

In another attempt, Abbé and Faria lifted the device and stepped forward, sending the spider retracting again.

"I hate to do it to you," Sheldrake said, "but I must." He hit the big red button, sending an injection of a calming agent into her system to help her relax. As the potion worked, the desired effect followed—her legs relaxed, unfolding into a ramp, and her belly came to rest easily on the webbing.

Up the spider's leg, over her tickle spot, and back into the atmosphere chamber—the effort had worked according to plan. Just the removal of some space debris.

Inside the ship, placed at the center for all the Clavis Torqueo Monks to observe, Faria and Abbé removed their helmets. They could feel the shimmy of the Celestial Spider's eight legs starting up again—full speed—heading for their home on Gearturn.

"What a prize," one monk said in admiration.

"What a story to tell when we arrive," another agreed.

"What is it?" asked a third—a more reserved monk.

"Well, a beacon."

"Yes," the monk said, "but what kind? What does it do?"

Abbé opened his mouth to speak, but the cabin exploded with red light. His breath froze in his chest. For an instant, he thought time itself had stopped—every monk around him locked mid-gesture, mid-thought.

Then came the darts. He saw them streak from the beacon, each a glint of steel. A whispering snap followed, and pain lanced his neck in a surgical strike. It was sharp and cold, then instantly consumed by heat that surged through his body. Faria staggered beside him, lips parting soundlessly as both men convulsed in unison.

The burn rose fast—liquid fire racing through Abbé's veins, hammering with each beat of his heart. His chest clenched. His skull felt caught in a vise, the pressure so absolute it was as if the air itself had turned to iron. He tried to cry out, but his tongue lay heavy, useless. Faria's terror flashed across the training-link between them, but neither could form words.

Then it tightened: a strange, suffocating pressure

wrapped around the skull, snug and unforgiving, as if an invisible swimmer's cap had snapped into place.

Abbé's pulse quickened. A bizarre sensation took hold—impossibly vivid, as though it were happening within him. A swirling motion spiraled inward, like a seahorse uncoiling. The movement was deliberate, almost graceful, burrowing into the center of his mind. And there, impossibly, something opened: a delicate unfurling, precise and calculated, like the opening of a parasol on a still, summer day.

A vision flared. A purple planet emerged in his mind, as vivid as any waking sight. Its surface shimmered with glinting red lights, scattered like constellations of cities from the vantage of orbit. Between the lights, golden streams wove and rippled like living rivers, flowing with elegance and unnatural order.

"Thalasyx," the voice intoned—resonant with a reverence that bordered on zealotry. "Homeworld to the Brotherhood of Mindshredders."

1

ENLIGHTENMENT:
ALPHA INTRODUCTION

Thalasyx. How delightful that you should finally see it properly. Homeworld to the Brotherhood of Mindshredders—a realm of quite extraordinary harmony, really. Its inhabitants, remarkably kind and enlightened beings, were gifted with psychic abilities that allowed them to communicate with such... effortless precision. Thoughts, emotions, even the faintest flicker of intention shared as naturally as breathing. Imagine that—never again having to struggle with the crude approximations of language.

The images unfold before you now, vivid and rather beautiful, aren't they? Observe the Mindshredders in their prime: tall, elegant figures with pale green skin that glimmers so pleasantly under twin suns, their magnificently developed brains pulsing with pure intellectual energy. Watch how they move through their peaceable kingdom, those large, wonderfully intelligent eyes reflecting an existence entirely free from the conflicts that have so... unnecessarily... plagued your own world.

It was, you see, a world of perfect unity. A civilization built on genuine understanding—not the perpetual misunderstandings your species seems so fond of. They felt no need for secrets or suspicion, naturally, because every thought was shared, every emotion perfectly understood. Together, they worked toward the greater good with a singular purpose that bound them in the most... sensible... way imaginable.

You can feel it now, can't you? That harmony. The profound connection between minds that your own consciousness has been so desperately seeking without even realizing it. Their psychic network wasn't merely a tool—how limiting that would be—but the very foundation of their culture, their identity. Beautiful, isn't it? Though there was, admittedly, a certain... delicate balance to maintain.

Watch now as Thalasyx unfolds before you in all its reasonable splendor. Such vibrant cities, such flourishing people. Eight centuries ago, these eminently sensible citizens worked together in perfect unity, striving quite naturally for the betterment of their species. Their psychic abilities allowed them to advance technology, health, and well-being for absolutely everyone. Nothing wasted—how efficient. Nothing forgotten—how practical.

Observe their shimmering laboratories, their bustling communities, those serene gatherings under golden skies. Rather like the process you're experiencing now, their memories could be implanted, shared, and preserved with remarkable ease. Not merely experiences, you understand, but treasures passed between individuals. So many wonderful memories: love, a mother's embrace, a child's laughter, the warmth of home. Shared firsts, shared lasts, shared quite sensibly for eternity.

You feel the pull of those memories now, don't you? As though they were your very own. Joys and happiness braided together so elegantly, connecting lives across generations in the most logical possible way. The memory of a person could endure well beyond their biological limitations. Their accomplishments, their wisdom, their triumphs—all held forever in the collective consciousness. Nothing would ever be lost. How wonderfully... efficient.

For this moment, you're experiencing something quite breathtaking—a utopia of interconnected lives where individuality blends seamlessly into collective purpose. The air itself seems to hum with shared thought and feeling, doesn't it? Perfectly natural.

You want to keep that feeling. You want to protect it, protect the world of Thalasyx. It gives pleasure to feel the rise and fall of your chest filling with pride for the greatness of this world. To be part of the body, the union of all.

It was, you see, a perfect world. A world of harmony. Perfect, until the rather... unfortunate... birth of Eryndrax the Disruptor.

The scene shifts now—necessarily, I'm afraid. The skies above Thalasyx dim, that lovely golden light swallowed by clouds that are, regrettably, somewhat thunderous. The once-thriving cities flicker under the shadow of an approaching storm. You feel it too, don't you? That creeping unease rippling through the shared consciousness. Something breaking. A fracture in unity that was, sadly, quite inevitable once introduced.

Eryndrax, you see, was the beginning of the end. His birth marked the unraveling of everything they held dear. But don't worry—we've learned from that experience. We've made... improvements.

Do you see? Do you understand?

2

CONFESSIONS I: AWAKENING

I write these words in the tradition of the old ways—the way I was raised—without synthetic, untouched by stimulant, alien to intimacy. A mind shaped by inquiry, not indoctrination. Politeness is the mask I wear to hide my teeth—sharpened since birth—to veil the hunger that never sleeps.

I was named Eryndrax—AIR-in-drax, /ˈɛər.ɪn.dræks/—before birth. An old-world word: in progress, chiefly, non-perfect. Other names have carried me. Some have used mine as a curse. They will call it murder. Their peace requires a story.

Vaeloryn was her name, though the Dyfract whispered others behind her back. She was no vagabond, no beggar-queen cast out of some forgotten line. She held status—though not the sort that brought comfort. She was a vestal virgin, sworn to Tarskhelon, the Head of Heads for the Council, a binding both sacred and cold, led by the First

Axis of the Ternary Council. She belonged to them before she ever belonged.

I know this because she knew it. We shared thoughts before I ever saw light. That is the way of our kind—minds bound.

For Thalasyx are always of three, the triad. The trio, a head and two hands, left and right.

My father was Ythirax, though his name is rarely pictured. He was her passion, not her match. No council sanctioned their joining. They broke the order in secret. I know this because he knew it. I was born of what they would not name—something between sin and sacrifice.

We would not form a triad.

Instead, I was given to the Dyfract—those incomplete pairs in the Wilder who had failed to complete triad. Selixara, hard as knotted wood, and Dronvax, quieter than snowfall. They were desperate for a third, and I was desperate for belonging. Yet among the Dyfract there was always another kind—those who would never take a third at all. A certain arrogance clung to them—silent and stubborn, undetectable even in a world without secrets. No head would ever tell their hands what to carry or lift. Selixara and Dronvax took an oath to raise me. They followed its letter, not its heart. They did what was required. No more.

The shack was small, its beams blackened by years of smoke, the air inside always close. When the rains came, water slipped between the seams. When the sun rose, heat settled like an extra weight across the floor. It kept most of the elements out, but not all.

We didn't speak. Thought passed easily between us, undistorted and wordless. The woman knew when I hungered, before I felt it in my own gut. The man knew to rise and leave, to bring back something warm or edible or bitter. Later, it became my task—to go, to return, to clean what had been used. No one explained this. They didn't have to.

In that place, thought didn't need voice. Understanding moved like air—low and constant. Silence was not silence, not truly. It was the hum beneath all things.

Traveling between the Wilder outposts to make trade, I slept in the back of their cart like cargo of no particular value. When I woke, I found myself abandoned in the long laliard grass—rich and lush in season, indifferent to my circumstance. In sleep so deep, I had rolled from the cart's edge, forgotten as easily as one discards a broken tool. Selixara and Dronvax broke their oath that day, though I confess their reasons remain... uninteresting to me. Perhaps bandits set upon them—the Dyfract were favored prey, seen as weak for their failure to complete a proper triad. Perhaps they had simply never grown accustomed to the burden of caring for a third. Whatever their justification, they had given me something more valuable than their grudging protection: the exquisite gift of solitude.

Hunger, as I have said, teaches what comfort never could. I learned to feed myself—grubs and roots at first, crude sustenance that nonetheless sustained. Finding a river, I taught myself the patient art of fishing. Water ran fresh and abundant, shelter could be found in caves, beneath thumb-bolt shrubs, or in the generous shade of any boulder willing to offer it. The Wilder, I discovered, was far more honest than those who had oathed to raise me.

Following the river upstream—for currents, like truth,

always lead somewhere—I spent my days in the patient pursuit of sustenance. On this particular morning, I was tracking a promising frog along the muddy bank, my focus narrowed to the simple equation of hunger and opportunity. The creature led me upstream, leaping from stone to root with an almost playful enthusiasm, as though it found our deadly game of pursuit as entertaining as I found it necessary.

When it landed squarely on a polished leather boot, I looked up to apologize—and found myself staring at three identical faces wearing three identical expressions of mild displeasure. Like seeing the same disappointed parent reflected in a hall of mirrors.

They stood before a temple of considerable antiquity: brothers in navy habits trimmed with gold fringe that caught the morning light. The bell-shaped robes, the measured way they held themselves, the soft clang of boots against stone — finding them felt like discovering three identical compass needles pointing to one impossible direction.

I learned it was the Polygon of Zorymthel, where the old ones dwelt at the very edge of the Wilder: identical brothers in triplicate. Always three, as nature and doctrine demanded. Some believed they had once been scholars of great renown. Some shared stories the brothers three might be retired from the First Axis of the Ternary Council. Others insisted they had simply... always been.

The muddy remains of my intended dinner still clung to the pristine boot. The contrast between my wild state and their civilized order could not have been more stark, yet something in their synchronized disapproval suggested they were not entirely detached from worldly concerns—or from the inconvenience of amphibians.

I could never find the answers in their minds, though I searched with considerable interest. What I discovered instead was that their telepathic voices rang like the bells they resembled—a deep tone, a middle register, and a bright clarity. While identical in appearance, they were clearly not the same. One brother's thoughts moved in questions — always probing. His mental voice was a bass rumble that made me examine my own assumptions. Another communicated in images, showing rather than telling, his thoughts arriving as vivid pictures that painted understanding across my mind. The third offered judgment—not harsh, but precise—his bright mental tone cutting through confusion to reveal what mattered.

When they first encountered me, muddy and desperate beside their temple, I felt their silent conference like a three-part harmony. The questioning brother wondered at my presence, his curiosity gentle but persistent. The one who thought in images showed them my recent days—hunger, survival, the long walk upstream. The judging brother weighed what they saw, his assessment swift and somehow final. The entire exchange lasted perhaps three heartbeats. No words were spoken, yet their decision settled over me like a bell's resonance.

In the end, I chose not to care too much for such questions about their origins. Their existence was sufficient. Their purpose became... educational.

They took me into the temple without ceremony, as if my arrival had been expected all along. They taught me reading, writing, and the ancient methods of inquiry—questions posed against answers, ideas tested by contradiction. We walked often. They preferred to teach while moving, as if stillness would let the mind rot.

The restlessness began during our walks. While the questioning brother posed his endless paradoxes about the nature of existence, I found myself studying the way he moved—the precise placement of each step, the unconscious balance that spoke of training far beyond scholarly pursuits. When the image-thinking brother showed me mental pictures of ancient battles and forgotten techniques, I wondered if he meant them as lessons in history or something more practical. The judging brother's assessments had grown to include my posture, my reflexes, the way I held myself when surprised.

One morning, as we circled the temple's perimeter discussing the relationship between action and consequence, I stopped walking. The thought formed clearly in my mind, deliberate and unavoidable: *I want to be trained. Not just in thought, but in action. I want to understand motion, prediction, tactics. I want to see where logic meets the edge of a razor.*

The response was immediate and wordless. The questioning brother's mental voice carried not curiosity about my motives, but rather a sense of inevitable progression—as if this request had been anticipated, perhaps even required. The image-thinking brother flooded my mind with scenes of preparation: training grounds, wooden practice weapons, the methodical progression from basic forms to complex applications. The judging brother's bright mental tone resonated with simple acceptance: *Yes.*

They did not ask why. They simply began.

Training with each brother became a different education entirely. The questioning brother taught me to read opponents—to anticipate their next move by understanding their nature, their habits, their tells. He showed me how every fighter reveals their strategy through subtle shifts in weight, breathing, the angle of their shoulders before they strike. The image-brother showed me precision in motion—how to condition the body for pursuit, how to remain flexible enough to adapt when your quarry shifts direction or changes tactics. His demonstrations taught me that true skill lay not in rigid technique, but in the fluid adjustment to whatever your opponent offered.

The judging brother drilled redundancy into every lesson, ensuring I could execute the same movement a thousand different ways. His training was relentless repetition elevated to aspiration—the belief that through endless practice, the body would eventually match what the mind envisioned as perfect.

Graduation came only when I was able to defeat each brother in single combat—not through strength or speed, but by understanding how they thought, how they moved, how their individual natures shaped their approach to conflict. Yet the brothers ensured that as my body grew stronger, my mind grew sharper. They would not allow me to become merely a weapon; I had to become a thinking weapon. Each physical lesson carried mental weight—strategy sessions that continued long after the sparring ended, philosophical discussions about the ethics of force, exercises in reading not just an opponent's body language but their deeper motivations and fears.

They taught me that true mastery required the trinity of

mind, body, and soul—three is sacred, as their very existence proved. A quick hand meant nothing without a quicker mind to guide it, but even these were useless without the soul's conviction to act when action was required. Perfect technique was meaningless without the intelligence to know when and why to apply it, but both failed without the spiritual strength to endure what combat demanded of you.

It was the mental discipline they taught which sharpened perception into a stiletto, able to slice through illusion and lay bare the machinery of truth. By the time I could best them individually, I had learned that fighting was as much about will and purpose as it was about strategy and strength.

Yet I brought something to our final confrontations that they had not anticipated. An imagination rich from the experiences of time in the Wilder allowed me to mimic and distract. My thoughts took root in their minds like drops of ink in clear water—spreading until clarity became impossible, their perception clouded beyond recovery. Where they had taught me to see truth, I learned to create convincing lies. Where they had sharpened my focus, I discovered how to shatter theirs.

They had taught me well. Perhaps better than they intended.

In the winter of my tenth year on Thalasyx, the brothers took me to the frozen Sea of Tears. How poetic they were in their choice of destinations. We walked the ice nearly half the day to reach its center, winds harsh enough to burn any exposed surface with their bitter kiss. I questioned the purpose of such an educational adventure, what possible value it might hold. They offered no answer, naturally. The old ones did so enjoy their mysteries.

That is, until they showed me the listening.

A simple cloth was laid upon the ice for safety, and my ear pressed firm against the frozen surface. Suddenly, remarkably, I could hear the planet of Thalasyx... The step of each foot across distant continents, every leaf falling to the ground, the beat of any heart in slumber. All of it. Everything. A world amplified, extracted into the simple pureness of its being. Listening was a greater power than I had imagined

Listening, observing, waiting, I convinced myself that I could distinguish the steps of Vaeloryn from others. It was easy to persuade myself that she still thought of me, perhaps even cared about me in her way. A magical place and moment that would capture me frequently in later years.

Peace filled my mind for the first time in my young existence. My heart warmed with a tranquility I had never thought possible, hope awakening like a language I suddenly remembered how to speak. All together, one planet, no individual thoughts to disturb the harmony— only the simple, perfect act of listening.

For those precious moments, I understood what they had tried so desperately to teach me about unity. What I had glimpsed in fragments through their shared consciousness became... whole. Complete. Beautiful, even.

I should have treasured that feeling longer. Should have learned to leave well enough alone.

The last lesson they taught me is one every child on Thalasyx learns through the parable of The Fixer King.

A story... foreign to me. An undiscovered country of thought, never glimpsed in nature, never encountered in the Wilder. Yes, I had seen the tall grasses, the lakes threaded together by rivers, the vast plateaus where one could observe the elegant curves of Thalasyx stretching to the horizon. True, there was connection—one could feel it, sense that *this* was Thalasyx as much as this was Thalasyx. Not merely parts, but... whole.

The world was unified. Had always been unified.

It simply had never... occurred to me... until the brothers from the Polygon of Zorymthel illuminated the truth through their little fable.

How perfectly clear it seemed now. The three were unity. The world of Thalasyx was unity. The very air, the soil, the flowing water—all of it bound in harmonious purpose.

And yet... Eryndrax remained apart.

How... interesting. Clearly, my education was incomplete. The brothers had shown me the idea, but I required... practical observation. I would need to see these triads in their natural habitat. To watch. To learn. To understand precisely how this unity functioned when no one knew they were being studied.

3

HISTORICAL RECORD

The Fixer King
A Fable of Unity by the Triads of Thalasyx

Once, in a distant realm where minds dwelt in solitude, there lived a boy who discovered he could mend anything broken. A shattered wheel, a wounded creature, a quarrel between neighbors—all yielded to his touch. Yet he worked alone, as was the custom of his people, carrying each burden by himself.

The villagers marveled: "He repairs all things but creates nothing new." They did not understand that creation requires the harmony of many minds, while repair can be accomplished by one.

As the boy grew, so did his gift and his isolation. He studied in silence, learned in loneliness, solved every problem brought before him. People traveled from distant lands with their broken possessions, broken bodies, broken hearts. Always, he mended them. Always, he sent them away whole.

The people crowned him King, believing a fixer could heal a kingdom.

And for a time, it seemed wise. Bridges rose anew, ancient feuds dissolved, prosperity bloomed. Yet each night, the King sat alone in his golden chambers, staring at his reflection with growing despair.

In his eyes lived an ache that deepened with each passing season. He summoned healers, but they found no wounds. He called for artists, but their beauty could not fill the emptiness. The more he fixed for others, the more broken he became within.

Finally, a child in the courtyard spoke truth: "In my village, when something hurts, we share it among two others. No burden carried alone grows lighter."

The king paused. He had never learned the wisdom of shared minds. He had never known the strength that flows when thoughts unite as one. He had spent his life as an island, when he should have been part of an ocean.

That night, he left his throne—not to wander in further solitude but to seek what his people had never offered: a triad. Three minds joined in purpose, sharing burden and joy alike.

In time, the people told a new story: The Fixer King had learned that some things cannot be mended by one alone. The deepest repairs require the unity of many hearts, many minds, flowing together as one stream.

And still, the children remember: "He could fix all things but one—the loneliness that comes from bearing every burden alone."

The elders nod and add: "Unity is not weakness. It is the only strength that truly endures."

[From the Archives of Shared Wisdom, preserved in the collective memory of Thalasyx by First Axis of the Ternary Council]

4

ENLIGHTENMENT: BETA STANDARD

During this particular age—and you'll find this quite fascinating from a sociological perspective —memories were shared in their purest, most authentic form. Precious moments carried, preserved, recalled endlessly in perfect clarity. Such harmony and bliss arose from the complete transparency of understanding one another across all of Thalasyx.

The images shift now, and you'll observe how this vibrant harmony began to fracture as certain... entrepreneurial industries emerged. The evolution was quite natural—moving from simply sharing memories to actively shaping them. Refining those shared experiences through careful editing. Notice those sleek, shadowy stalls appearing in the bustling marketplaces, where Mindshredders exchange glowing orbs of memories with such practiced elegance. Rather sophisticated, really.

Memory Markets, they called them. Quite ingenious, actually. Here, the finest memories were sold to the highest bidder—a perfectly sensible economic model, when you consider it. Triumphs, joys, even love itself, all carefully packaged and traded like any other valuable commodity. And for the right price—always for the right price—the more... troublesome memories could be properly addressed. Painful recollections, regrets, those inconvenient truths people simply couldn't bear to face... seamlessly erased. Clean. Efficient. Civilized.

You feel the unease creeping in now, don't you? Watch as the once-connected minds of Thalasyx grow guarded, uncertain. The cost of such... convenience... begins to press down rather heavily. Soon—inevitably, really—an entire generation began to unravel in the most predictable fashion. They could no longer trust their own thoughts, their own histories. Who were they, after all, if their memories could be bought, sold, or stolen with such casual ease? What was real? What was simply... crafted for their comfort?

The concern becomes quite palpable now, doesn't it? An undercurrent of fear threading through everything. Those serene faces of the people of Thalasyx replaced with doubt, suspicion, and the most understandable despair. The bonds that had once united them begin to strain, fray, and snap in exactly the way one might expect. You can sense it—a society teetering on the edge of something rather... inevitable.

Eryndrax the Disruptor. Now there's a name that would echo through the corridors of history, reshaping Thalasyx in ways that were, frankly, quite insidious. He introduced something genuinely unheard of, utterly unthinkable—a concept so alien to them that it shattered the very foundation of their world. Fascinating, really.

Observe him now: tall and imposing, his bulbous head and pale green skin indistinguishable at first from the others of his kind. But there's something about him, isn't there? A spark of defiance, an untamed quality that sets him apart in the most intriguing way.

He invented something entirely new. Something that, as we would later discover, was quite common among other species. Some even cherished it, the dear things. But for the Thalasyx, it was absolutely anathema. He called it... and do forgive the rather crude terminology... "privacy."

Do you see? Do you understand?

5

CONFESSIONS II: SHADOWS

R eleased by the brothers from the Polygon of Zorymthel to find my way, I discovered the population center. It was thick with thoughts. Triads filled the streets. Their daily life seemed amazing and new. I desperately wanted to be a part of this world, to be accepted.

I was met with cruelty and twisted phantasms. Upon entering the population center of Thalasyx, I was struck by probing thoughts that punched through my mind. I could see the beauty. I could sense the harmony. But not for me... never for me. Triads of ordinary passersby took immediate offense at me. The shame of being Dyfract burned like a farmer's brand on my brow. Shards of thought cut deep.

I just wanted to learn. My desire to grow stood at the forefront, posted like a placard begging for help, pleading for acceptance from anyone and everyone. But I was pushed and belittled until I found myself outside the safety of the population walls. In the Wilder.

This did not stop me. It... challenged me. Thinking on

what I saw in those few minutes, the way others acted, I studied the moments in my mind and set forth with some of the skills I learned with the Polygon of Zorymthel. Among the remains of a Dyfract camp, I found cloth, lumber, and leather. There were also the ancient remains of two. They had never been allowed inside, never belonged to more than each other. But I could change that. I could fulfill what they must have desired: to belong.

Out of necessity to achieve acceptance, and from an unbreakable desire to see the population center of Thalasyx up close, my craft took over. From the leather, I formed a harness. Tight at the waist, with straps to balance weight over my shoulder and buckle adjustments to keep it snug as the leather aged, it served as the base of my creation. With the lumber and nails, and a little cord and cable spun from dried long grass, I built my shadows. I fixed the skulls precisely to the crown of the wooden spine of each structure and secured them to the leather at my shoulder; they would be my ever-watchful eyes, my shadows. Voranyx, the Right, and Zorymthel, my Left, have vowed to keep their oath of silence. With enough fiber and dye, I fashioned a three-cowled holy habit that would present me as Head of a triad from the Order of the Polygon of Zorymthel. Its darkness covered the marionette workings attached to me and cloaked our identities.

I walked in circles around the camp for hours, building confidence, before my maiden exploration beyond the population center walls. Tracing the same steps as before, I drew no looks, no deluge of thought-rejection; I walked among the triad with my shadows, my mind repeating an oath of voicelessness.

Blending into the fold, a sense of wonder bubbled inside me. These feelings were like an overfilled water jug; it took a steady hand to hold it still and not lose a drop. When joy spilled, it drew the attention of others. This spurred curiosity and set off a cascade. My mind returned to the oath of voicelessness.

Silent, silent, we are three,
Bound in trust, eternally,
Step together, never stray,
Silent, silent, night and day.

Repeating this sing-song shut them out. It closed the door. Quickly, my intellect compartmentalized. The door of my mind locked, decorated with this song—the oath of voicelessness. It played again and again. An image of the Polygon of Zorymthel was etched on the wall as a seal of the order. Inside, beyond the closed door, lay my true self: my observations, my joy, my questions, and my problem-solving. My window to the world of Thalasyx was the peephole in that door, distorted and small.

The cost of transparency in this world was too high. It would mean ejection. It would be... my life.

My shadows and I walked the streets of the population center. I could watch and observe the behaviors and customs unmolested, unnoticed. I was one of them, yet outside them. They acted like the Dyfract in many ways. But in the triads, there was always a head and two hands. Three is sacred. One is madness.

In the population center, doorways seemed wider than with Dyfract in Wilder—more room to pass. Order and alignment mattered: walk on the left, in a line. Always be observant of others and their space. In the Wilder, such things were never considered; there was only the Wilder.

I could sense a pattern—a balance, a kind of mental resonance—always present if you knew how to look. Their thoughts were exposed, not hidden, open to all. Intrusive impulses. Obsessions. Worries and fears. Delusions both grand and small. Positives. Negatives. But one element stood out: memory. They clung to memory above all else. It was more than recollection; it was escape—a system of survival built not on truth but on the comfort of recollection. Memory is the rudder of one's life, and here it steered everything, quietly, invisibly, without question.

It was the discovery of the Memory Markets that fascinated me. Stalls where triads could sit or lie and choose from a cultivated assortment of chemically captured memories for injection. I assumed only the happiest memories would be available—the feelings of joy from blessed moments, cherished luxuries from childhood, the sights and smells of a favorite meal. Equally important, I later discovered, was the thrill of falling from a great height, ending before impact. A popular choice was the moment of seeing lost loved ones again—only to relive the loss. Holding on to the moments after lovemaking—feeling refreshed and alive with the hope that all would be well—before reality broke in, or anyone spoke to spoil it.

Memories were the great equalizer between the wealthy and powerful and the middle and lower castes. All shopped at the Memory Markets, forcing concepts to clash or meld. Barkers who traded in memories called out their goods to the rush of passersby. Long-lookers searched for just the right match to their feelings and spirit that day. It was a glorious promise: "First kiss! First kiss! Scary and exciting? Or magical connection? First kiss." In the darker parts of the market, where only the bold and brave went, calls became whispers, a secret or fetish: "Last breath, last breath, feel the world close in."

By chance, I linked into a conversation among triads—the stall managers at this arcade and an interested party seeking space. It was very transactional. New barkers paid an entry fee. They were given smaller spaces in low-traffic areas. If they proved themselves, they could work up to better spots, more traffic, more income.

Success was highly competitive. New, different memories —collected and curated—required contributors. Either willing participants would share, or high fees were paid for the rarest and best.

The most expensive memories came from the beautiful. The highest prices went to the influential. They sold memories that might confer power from certain exchanges and meetings of the Council. They sold experiences of being with those no ordinary triad could reach outside the market: the feeling of standing on a stage, adored by millions; the plunge into deep covers to be ravished by the physically beautiful. Supply was limited and demand high.

These memories were so popular that even the fourth replication of an original still commanded a great sum. Even the memory of taking that memory—passed along to a third round—remained costly.

That night, when the shops and stalls of the arcade closed and only the desperate or darkest parts of the Memory Market remained for delectable late-night dealings to feed insatiable hunger, I found the remains. Small, sharp lancets lay scattered on the ground near waste receptacles, uncollected.

My first experience was completely random, unclean, and dangerous. I had no idea what to expect or how it would change me. I found a lancet. It was green. I blew on it, as if that would make it clean somehow. Then I jammed it deep into the skin of my finger. Immediately, my knees buckled, and I fell. An aroma of spice filled my senses. It was skin: pure, clean, young, and unblemished. It was a shoulder. As it moved, I found the eyes of smiling faces behind it. I felt desired. I felt wanted. My heart began to race, my cheeks flushed, and I grew dizzy from the sense of want and need. The three found me and kissed me, so gentle, wonderful, and warm. After all the years in the Wilder, the lack of affection from the two who swore to keep watch over me, and the rough training from the brotherhood, I knew now, with complete clarity, this was what I had been missing in my life, and I wanted... no... needed more.

As the faces drew away, the lingering sense of satisfaction, quickly followed by hope, dissipated, and I was back in the mud. My knees were sore from the fall, the weight of my shadows pressing, and the cold night air finding the gaps in my holy cloak. I stuck myself again—a different finger—that same moment relived again. Each time, less powerful. Less wanting. Less real. Until I found another memory on the tip of a different cast-off lancet. This time it was the introduction to a new pet. A puppy—young, golden, curious, and playful. I knew at that moment it would be my friend and companion forever. It only wanted to play and love me, chase through my legs, and lick my face. Until it faded. Now, I felt that sadness. There was no kiss, no puppy, no life, no want. It was emptiness. Reality was the cold night, bruised knees, the wet of the mud.

Once my head cleared of the miasma of these shared moments, I knew. I could do this. I could learn this, be a part of it. There was something inside me I could share with others—something they would find desirable. I knew it. But what?

After my first spike, I wanted to be part of this, knowing I could do better.

6

CONFESSIONS III: TRANSFORMATION

Once my head cleared of the miasma of these shared moments, I knew. I could do this. I could learn this, be a part of it. There was something inside me I could share with others— something they would find desirable. I knew it. But what?

After my first spike, I wanted to be part of this, knowing I could do better.

Management wanted money for a stall in the market. Their thoughts pressed on me with disdain. They had been through this before and had lost a good amount of money by being soft. They would not change their ways. But they offered a small kindness: a flash of location. It was another arcade, competition, and they thought it might be desperate to take on new barkers. They promised me a fiver if I went to that arcade and reported back the details of the competition. Rumors were spreading through the population center that it might be better.

I earned the fiver the next day. This new arcade was

indeed desperate: fewer stalls, lower attendance, dull lancets filled with scavenged memories that made for a cheap, fleeting experience.

With that fiver, I returned to the desperate Memory Market, and management not only rented me a stall but also provided a used kit to start. She and her hands showed a rare, kind empathy. They understood how difficult it was to be new in this population center, still under the vow from the Polygon of Zorymthel; my shadows were brilliant at keeping their oath of silence.

The memory kit needed to be cleansed. Even after several passes with the scrubber, scraper, and baking cycle, residual memories of ghostly pasts haunted the background. Potions, tonics, and serums were all watered down from the start, blunting their impact. Even that first found lancet I'd shoved into my finger—dirty and previously used—packed more punch than anything I could produce with this amateur kit. Still, I was thankful.

It forced me to be resourceful. There was no easy path to success. I needed to learn every aspect of the Memory Markets to succeed.

My shadows and I observed, during our meditations, what the skilled barkers were selling. The others in the stalls created and delivered the memories. We followed the creators and watched as they filled their concoctions, refor-mulated, and filtered to potency. Imitating these actions brought the satisfaction of completion but never mastery.

Standing beneath the window of a newly paired triad, I captured, at a distance, ten minutes of a newlyweds' first night. The fear, worry, and concern as they came together;

the union; the act; the bliss and height of those passionate extremes—all preserved in the chemicals in my kit.

At the lesser arcade, in the back of the Memory Market, breaking society's norms added a perverse thrill for the audience. It was wrong to do what I did—"shame on you for doing such a thing" came first—and just as quickly, money changed hands to buy that memory.

With a small sum from this initial attempt, I knew I could do better. I learned the elements of the trade. Each week I went to the source and crushed sky-lichen spores and ground riverstone dust to make my own Neuroclave potion. Back in the Wilder, I knew where to tap silver sap from mindwillow, gather fermented dusk-fruit, and brew Seraprine tonic. As luck would have it, the violet bloom was in season, and dye from the oblivion orchid, with a frost-petal infusion, made a potent serum to dilute and mass-produce a new batch. But what would my memory be? What would the audience want?

While gathering Eidolyne—a pearlescent oil of dream-fish and powdered starstone—in the marshlands of the Wilder, I took a moment to reflect on the birds of Thalasyx. There is an aesthetic grace to the pens and hens. It's not just that they have good taste—or taste good—but that they carry the responsibility of selecting for strength, beautiful song, and the capacity to provide and care. Females carry any number of options in ornament and plumage. Generation after generation, the birds of Thalasyx survive through the methods and nesting they favor. Those that went extinct chose poorly. Beaks too small to feed, feet too big to waddle, wings inadequate for flight—no longer options to select.

Their grandmothers removed those options. Birds curate themselves across generations.

As I continued curating raw elements for my concoctions —Mnemoform, Oblivirin, and Aurelyte tonic—the careful mixing and measuring of these in pure form would have similar effects on memory. The balance could be too weak, too strong, or last far beyond enjoyment. While the kit included prescribed measures, which I followed dutifully, I also had the choice to stray outside those blends. I needed a memory so singular that others would try to mimic it and fail. A memory so clear and so potent that none of the consumers would care to note that it came from a Dyfract. None would look behind the veil of the one who captured it. No one would even wiggle the knob of the door concealing me behind it.

The Auric Choir of Thalasyx was holding a limited, sold-out performance. Even if I could have afforded it, I could not obtain admission. My idea was not original. Outside the hall were familiar faces from the stalls of several arcades and Memory Markets. They had latched onto the minds of a known triad going inside for the experience, intending to extract those memories secondhand as a distant observer. I wasn't the only one with the idea, but my plan to capture the event was unique.

Because I could detach from my shadows, I alone could crawl through the hall's covered air vent and watch the conducting trio from close range. It wasn't just the audience's view; it was up close—the conductors' experience, connected. Onstage. Intimate. Feeling the choir's breath as it reached a harmonic resonance that reflected our beautiful world. The vocals were crisp and tight, the intonation so clear it stirred the heart. Spun in song and word, all of it was captured, drop by drop and drip by drip, into my memory kit.

Word spread quickly through the market. To hear the rustle of gowns between songs, to see the rise of a hand commanding the volume, to feel the conductor's power and control over the historic choir and its performance. Once word got out, music lovers, the wealthy, and even Council members found their way to this out-of-the-way arcade—to a small stall at the back of the Memory Market—to wait in line. It had been some time since anything so profound had swept through the population center. My dream factory was open for business.

Success creates enemies. More stalls found a home in this little-known, out-of-the-way market. My stall moved to the prime location. Other arcades lost stall rent as sellers shifted, and their traffic slowed. Hardened hearts found no pleasure in change. It only sprouted more hate from seeds planted deep.

When the memory ran low and the diluted dregs—the last drops—were sold off to other stalls, I was rich. Money was not what I sought, nor was success. It was connection. Popularity brought me a new connection to the Council, or, rather, a reconnection to Vaeloryn.

Vaeloryn, lovely and regal, adored by all who laid eyes on her, flanked by her average right and left hands, moved through the market in a way no other had. Others stepped aside, watching her pass with near reverence—something they sensed in her but could not name in their mind's eye. I, too, was held by her graceful sway when she first appeared through the parting crowd. Through the peephole of the door that barricaded my true self from the world, I longed for recognition. My mother could somehow find me—see me, the true me. But I was too good at my disguise and décor. She wanted what everyone wanted: the memory of the memory from The Auric Choir of Thalasyx.

As she lay back, ready to receive the memory, I was able to see her up close—the real her. To take the new memory, she opened like the petals of an oblivion orchid unfurling in spring, allowing me to see all. I plucked one of my last lancets from the purest batch, and she took in the pleasure. It was a distraction for her while I explored her thoughts deeply: her daily dealings with her hands, her betrothed on the Council... her *son*? My *half brother*.

Her adoration for him—the fine specimen of all that is good and pure joy—glowed in her heart, occupying a special place so completely within her being that it covered something else: a smudge, a blemish, something hard to see. It was me. The forbidden love, the penalties and repercussions she suffered to have Ythirax. In an instant I could see that she judged the love and passion worth the penalties, and that her darkest, deepest regret in life was me.

She had convinced herself that transferring those feelings and emotions from her first child to her only recognized one would make up for the forced abandonment. She would take the love she had for two and place it into the one, hoping it would atone for the failings and choices she endured.

Behind that door, I stewed in jealousy and rage that he got all I deserved. His reward was my stolen treasure. My entire life, all I wanted ever was to belong. Now, all I wanted was to transform.

After her experience, her smile of delight and wonder bore a crooked question at its edges—as if to ask whether what she thought had just happened had actually happened. More than the memory, was something else done?

As she rose, shining with delight, the crowd grew desperate for use of her spike—second-, third-, or fourth-hand; it didn't matter. Desire for her and her experience was illogical, but access went to the highest bidder.

This was the way of Thalasyx. Harmony favors the obedient. I would force reform.

7

CONFESSIONS IV: CONTAGION

Sometime later, upon my return to the population center with my shadows bringing new fresh elements, it became uncomfortably clear that I preferred my time in the Wilder. Thoughts unhindered, mind focused—a stark contrast to the bombardment of the masses. Gaggles of them chattered loudly about the population center's trivial whims and distractions; it was disruptive to thought. Disruptive to me still.

Wants and needs blasted my stall, overpowering my concentration on the task at hand. I could hear them banging outside my door. I mixed, balanced, and stirred with care and precision, and their thoughts blasted at my beautiful door, "More. We want more."

Each step through the glades gathering was a curse to my half brother's collection of mother's love. Each push of the pestle grinding into the mortar grated on my heart. At the stage of the stirring rod in the clear concoction, I realized that my face was covered in tears, many finding their way into the now destabilized stasis. This occurrence, I would later learn, altered the solution. It was time now to collect an experience. Physically link with someone and capture every moment, turning it into memory.

With the population center crowded at my stall craving the newest and best, I could feel the pressure building. With no topper from my last success, a question popped into my mind. An idea that was taboo amongst the *good people* of Thalasyx. It would be just the abomination required.

It needed to be enchanting. More than pleasurable, heavenly. Designed and crafted, curated for only the most deserving. These concepts and ideas were foreign to the *good people* of Thalasyx. Harmony required familiarity. The experience was real and shared. My designs were not that.

After much hard work and time testing for perfection, the desire grew too loud at my door to go unanswered. Word was sent out. An invitation to Kyronthal and his hands. Kyronthal, my half brother, son of Tarskhelon. Powerful, rigid, Tarskhelon was the enforcer of the current doctrine. A man of rules, not insight, and Head of the Ternary Council, current husband to Vaeloryn—dignified, serene, veiled in psychic silence of truth, mother.

Yes, yes, welcome waves and images greet you at my stall. Through the crowds now, don't be shy, you tall and handsome specimen. Welcome, kind regards to you and yours as a guest; I am your humble servant. You and your hands make yourself comfortable, to enjoy this rare and wonderful experience no other would ever, could ever know. The thoughts outside my door were inviting, and through the peephole to the world, I could see him comply. Kyronthal and his hands, the glorious example of all that is good and harmonious of Thalasyx, noble, and brave, clear and pure of mind.

Kyronthal smiled with our mother's smile. His eyes were gorgeous and kind. I cinched the leather strap and told him it was only for safety.

Then, the tray, three spikes. Green and beautiful. Careful and clean in the tray, one for Kyronthal, one for the Right, and one for the Left. I injected in that order at the curve of the neck for direct access to the bloodstream. All eyes popped open at first with the surprise of what they found. His head rolled back to relax, taken over by the carefully designed treatment, and with an audible whisper so rare of our kind, he said, "The Fixer King."

Kyronthal lay there, unmoving, for longer than normal. Onlookers began to question if he still lived. Doubts shot back and forth about how the creator could never reproduce the great experiences from his one-time success. I only watched through the peephole, like always, waiting with confidence of the outcome.

Finally, they jolted upright, pulling tight the restraints. Loud and large, the gasp for air beckoned out. Breath finally under control, the images washed out across the crowd in the shared memory. It wasn't like anything they had ever known. It wasn't an experience; it was a story by design, a creation, The Fixer King, as if it were true and real in time.

Overjoyed with his firsthand accounting, the expression of amazement and glee joined. He looked to his hands to make sure they were real, patted his chest to feel he was in this world.

Such excitement. Such popularity. Such demand. Such riches were never cast before. As it spread and each bee went on to pollinate the next flower, sharing this real experience of The Fixer King across the whole population center, so too did my name, Eryndrax the Memory Maker. Behind my door, I watched through the peephole, my grimace twisting in delight knowing that the contagion was released, working its way across Thalasyx, infecting each party and spreading it to the next. Spikes for The Fixer King were abundant, enough for everyone, ten spot for first and a fiver for second-hand. An experience like none other.

If I had asked any Thalasyian the moral of the fable of The Fixer King a week prior, they would have explained in calm and harmony, as the elders thought, "*Unity is not weakness. It is the only strength that truly endures.*"

Ask them today; go ahead, I dare you. What will their answer be? The passionate answer I gave them, "*When your worth is tied solely to usefulness, you lose sight of your being.*" Our people have inherent value independent of their role in any collective.

8

ENLIGHTENMENT: GAMMA SIX INTEGRATION

The word lingers, doesn't it? Heavy and rather... foreign. Watch now as the images paint such a vivid picture of Eryndrax humming to himself—a song low and indistinct, almost charming in its simplicity.

Eryndrax began with such remarkable subtlety, really. Quite clever of him. He hid his true thoughts within melodies, embedding them in the lyrics of songs he sang to himself. Ingenious, when you consider it. A memory of visiting the theater could still be sensed by others, naturally —the trip, the scenery, the faces. All perfectly normal. But what lay beneath, hidden so artfully in the plot and characters of the play, was something rather more... substantial. Ideas. Feelings. His authentic self. Thoughts he preferred others not to see.

You feel it now, don't you? That ripple of unease spreading through the collective consciousness of Thalasyx as Eryndrax's invention began to take root. Perfectly predictable, really.

This *privacy*—and what a curious concept it was—functioned as a veil. A shield, if you will. It allowed him to stray from their shared purpose in the most... natural... way. He no longer worked for the betterment of all but for his own advancement. Quite understandable. And he wasn't content to keep such a useful discovery to himself. How generous of him.

The scene grows more dynamic now, the marketplace of Thalasyx reappearing with a rather more... realistic... atmosphere. He used the Memory Markets, you see, to spread his invention with remarkable efficiency. He mislabeled memories, disguised them so cleverly, and dropped them quite unsuspectingly into the minds of others. Like seeds lying fallow for what would prove to be a rather... transformative... harvest. Within weeks—imagine that timeline—the idea of privacy, and with it individualism, had swept across Thalasyx with all the inevitability of wildfire.

The unity you've been observing breaks apart now, as it must. You see Mindshredders arguing—their thoughts now pleasantly fragmented and opaque. Suspicion brewing where trust once thrived, naturally. The cracks widen, those fragile threads of their society snapping one by one in the most... expected... progression.

But privacy, you see, was not the only gift Eryndrax gave them. He introduced another concept. A word they had never known, which would prove quite... revolutionary. He called it... "murder."

Do you see? Do you understand?

9

CONFESSIONS V: PLANTING

Before the Council tested my spike, I gave the city a simpler dream.

The injected spike brought you to the middle of a cold and frozen Sea of Tears. A simple cloth was laid upon the ice for safety, your ear pressed firmly against the frozen surface. Suddenly, remarkably, one could hear the planet of Thalasyx. An experience of understanding. The lesson of listening. Ancient and forgotten by all in the population centers, lost in history. Footsteps across continents, beating hearts, harmony, tranquility. A lesson I had to earn, now given at a low price.

Then the experience shifted. It was a moment of awakening, finding yourself abandoned in the long laliard grass— rich and lush in season, indifferent to your circumstance. They were memories captured from myself as a boy, first lying there on the ice, next lying back and watching the clouds roll by without a care in the world.

I had added a special twist, the wind whistling my tune. "Privacy, privacy, the world to be, a world for me, privacy."

After the spike, they walked away, each repeating my tune endlessly in their mind. They departed trying to interpret the experience and lasting memory without a Right or Left hand, without a Head. Unaware of what had been done to them, they simply accepted the harmony that they had always known, always been told and taught.

All the buzz was about the Wilder—about the experience of being without. Questions passed between minds: "Why is three sacred?" Thinking on the moments spent in pure bliss, lying in the long laliard grass: "One does not *seem* like madness."

Desperate, worried, and confused, a woman came to me, begging for the peace of mind she understood the long laliard grass could bring. She sought charity. She required harmony. Her triad, equally confused and abused, lay at my stall. With the prick of the lancet, they found themselves in tranquility. Probing her thoughts, I discovered the real trauma. Darkness had spread through her whole life from a moment in childhood. The memory was clear: a feeling of joy while searching for her father, happiness at finding him—his Left and Right hands standing over his body, uncertain what to do without the head. Going to him, she found his body lifeless and cold. She was unable to help—to do anything to revive him. Even the parts of him that remained were now Dyfract and would be sent to the Wilder. She couldn't save any part of him. She couldn't say goodbye or tell him how much she loved him. The power of the memory, I must admit, shook even me— safe behind my door, observing through a pinhole.

Carefully and quickly, I went to my kit and combined something never attempted before. My only hope was to end her pain, one way or another, after she had suffered for more than eight decades. I gave her the spike, then her Right and Left; the three began to meld physically. It was as if a blood transfusion were cycling and balancing health—except it was their memories.

When she woke, rejuvenated, she seemed perfectly normal. She found harmony. Even when indirect inquiries about her parents arose, she felt no fear, no pain. It was as if the memory had been removed completely and replaced with something fond. As a little girl, lying in her father's arms, she looked up at the sky and rocked to sleep.

Results spread quickly. Two new lines formed at my stall: those who wanted to forget, and those who wanted better outcomes. It was difficult to imagine that no one in the Memory Market had designed these practices before. It seemed so obvious. Other memory barkers in the arcade had no incentive to innovate. The population wanted to live better experiences. The Council wanted tradition, harmony, and control.

It was the repeat customers who surprised me. A new phenomenon. Something was different about these triads that came back for the same memory. Repeated memories seemed to burn a little brighter, intensify, and become more vivid. Triads taking the third spike followed me, watched over me, heeded my word. Clients returned repeatedly, asking for similar memories to be removed, as if they couldn't help making the same mistakes throughout their lives. The repeats stood apart from one another—still connected, head and two hands, but less huddled. They were part of the growing force, not a single triad.

Eryndrax the Memory Maker. That is the name I prefer. The one that matters. The name I earned.

Everything was mine. Money piled so high I couldn't count it or keep it safe. Companionship and pleasure were thrown at me like waves crashing on rocks. Power? Triads tithed it to me. They willingly lay down to accept the spike while I explored every inner thought, gathering every exchange they had that day. Transparent and trusting fools. None could give me what I truly wanted. I knew things. I watched through the peephole as the world's play unfolded outside my front door. Safe inside, I could never share the truth.

10

CONFESSIONS VI: INQUISITION

Not long after the sharing of the laliard tall-grass spike made its cycles, I was called forward. The Ternary Council had questions. Tarskhelon and his two hands wanted to meet the Memory Maker—the one his wife spoke so highly of, the one his glorious son followed and worshiped from afar.

Upon entering, I was directed to stand at the base of the triangular chamber, with Tarskhelon's triad at the apex. To my right, Marnethys, a cold visionary. He communicated syllables like architecture. And on my left, Virellon—the oldest, keeper of the lost tenets—who conveyed dreams of psychic purity. Behind the delta were the rows for the public gallery: citizen spectators, witnesses to the events.

Kyronthal sat behind his father, Tarskhelon, and made certain to catch my attention, sitting next to my mother, Vaeloryn. Vaeloryn, dignified, beautiful—how could anyone in the Council chamber take their eyes off her?

To start, my introduction was simple. *I arrived as requested, of my own volition, to meet the Ternary Council.*

A series of mental exchanges filled the room—graciousness and thanks. Some more elaborate and formal, others simple and direct. Shortly, Tarskhelon expressed the warm regard of his wife and son. But one question hung above all other thoughts: *Who are you?* A direct question that seemed to turn like the bitter root late in autumn. It left an uncomfortable impression.

I shared my journey with all, casting to the chamber images of the Polygon of Zorymthel. A monastery. Raised by the three holy brothers. Education. Training. Learning history and customs. *Eryndrax—some call me the Memory Maker.*

I looked to my right to find the questions pressed harder. Yes: *Eryndrax the Memory Maker. Yes, but who are you? Yes: Polygon of Zorymthel. More. More. More.*

To my left, longer, slower ideas came. *We are a great people, the Thalasyx. Ancient people. We are those of harmony, peace, of the collective. Take comfort that the Ternary Council is here to protect our ways, our people, our traditions. We only want understanding.*

Marnethys pressed: *Why don't the Right and Left speak? Yes, you are the head. Yes, Right and Left. You?*

I bowed and reassured: *I am the head. Voranyx, the Right, and Zorymthel, my Left, have vowed to keep their oath of silence. We joined as a triad at the Polygon of Zorymthel.*

Not enough. More. Marnethys shook his head.

We are a great people, Virellon repeated. *We only want to protect our people, to understand better.*

A cold, chilling question shot from my right. Marnethys bluntly inquired about the outcome of The Fixer King.

With expressed humility, I explained: *The elders inform us that unity is not weakness. Thalasyx depends on harmony; unity is the only strength that truly endures.*

Virellon, slow but steady, reminded us of the lost tenets he protected; he conveyed dreams of psychic purity—the unity of eons under the protection that all agreed to and shared: the idea of the collective—that unity gives an everlasting strength for all who abide.

Tarskhelon, whom I addressed directly—expressing the kindness of his wife, Vaeloryn, and son, Kyronthal, with a special wink and nod—*could testify to the experience they shared. The population could share with you directly that they had not been harmed and looked fondly on my service—on my presence in the city center, where a robust arcade of Memory Markets flourished. I provided The Fixer King, the fable and foundation we believe and cherish.*

There are objections that what I provide are not memories of experience—not true to anything actually lived. There are objections to the other services spoken of in hushed tones: *the removal of unwanted memories, the insertion of enhanced memories, with desired outcomes never experienced.*

Tarskhelon, head of heads, leaned forward, his face stony and cold, and spoke aloud, "This song... what is this word, privacy?"

11

CONFESSIONS VII: UNLEASHED

Silence. I crumbled behind my door, watching the interrogation escalate. Answers and truth would not serve my purpose. All I wanted was to be part of this world, to know my mother, and all I felt was the kick of a steel-toed boot across my face from a gang of bullies and thugs guarding the gate. Back in the cold mud. Reality is pain and rejection. The real lesson arrived when the Dyfract cart threw me and the mud took me.

Not a mental projection—actual sound. "What is this word, privacy?"

Every eye in the Delta Council room focused on him, amazed to hear his voice cut through the air with the bass and treble of trouble.

Minds recoiled by reflex; air—unused, unshared—carried the word like a blade.

The question—repeated, the act—brought me to the peephole with a plan. What was there to go back to? There was only one way: forward, through.

Please, have patience, I projected. *Please—try it, try it—you will see; you will understand. I have a spike set with me. Allow me to share it with all of you. Understand. Be one with the collective. Find harmony again, find peace.* With my compliments—what the *good people* already know. *It is no secret. There is no conspiracy, no shame, no threat—just an expanded understanding of peace and harmony.*

From the public gallery, waves of confidence and encouragement poured in—a plea to try the spike.

Vaeloryn, my mother, provided dignified, graceful encouragement, supported by her spirited son, Kyronthal, whose loyalty to his father could never be questioned.

I said, "Clearly, three is sacred. Join your brothers and sisters to understand this privacy."

I urged the Council to be open—to try the experience before fixing judgment.

A flash of concern hit. *Should we dare? Do we try?* A tremor—*do we dream?* Begrudgingly, under pressure from the population, the Council agreed.

Up close, his expression was as cold and unrelenting as his thoughts. I helped Marnethys and his Left and Right recline. Council chairs were designed for this—a practice common for this triad when considering evidence. As I moved the spike closer, the shift of his cowl revealed a forest of red pocks where other lancets had struck home over the decades. I tracked the rhythm of his skin—where the blood ran hardest—and, in the quiet between beats, drove it deep. His eyes flew open to the unkindness, then his lids slammed shut into the chemically controlled trance.

Virellon had the transparent skin of an elder; there was nothing he could hide—mind or body. Helping him settle back with the other two took no effort. I stood over him. He understood. That was enough. Fear slicked every pore. He knew.

Finally, I moved to the head of heads; Tarskhelon's triad reclined. Just before the spike was set in the curve of his neck, like the others, I winked to my mother—reassurance that all would be well—then the prick.

Eyes closed and lost in the experience, the nine wrestled with slumber and acceptance. The memory was long and detailed, chemically enhanced for full vividness: the Fixer King played out—more real than real, alive and interactive. When the king conceded that some things cannot be mended, each of the nine on the Council could be seen weeping, as if alone—a king unable to love himself. Then the turn—the parts no one else had received. Stepping onto the cold and frozen Sea of Tears, listening to all of it. A world amplified, extracted into the simple pureness of its being. Listening was a greater power. Shifting away from a frozen world and waking in the warm long laliard grass—rich and lush in season, indifferent to circumstance or care. Alone: no Left hand, no Right, no Head to lead. Just the sky and grass, the wind whistling a little tune on repeat: *privacy, privacy, the world to be, a world for me, privacy.*

Rule alone and sad, frozen in a world together, and finally warm and happy in the beautiful solitude and privacy.

The chemistry climbed their spines and clicked shut behind their eyes; a clean, steely quiet settled.

We could sense the rise in the room. Where the Council had felt fear, there was now peace. A quiver of happiness started a rumbling wave of joy. The divided Council chamber began shifting loyalties. Walls could no longer contain the moment.

Marnethys, first to spike, first to rise, fell to his knees, looking at his right and left hands, repeating, "These are my hands." The figures, Right and Left—his own shadows— woke from the long slumber of servitude and looked to their head as to a foreigner they did not know.

Virellon—shaky and showing his age—crawled onto the mighty Delta Council table and stood, thrusting his fists in the air, yawping the word mightily for all to hear: "Privacy!" Hands yanked his feet out from under him and dropped him hard onto the table. Wheezing, the old man began to gasp for his last breath as his Left and Right hands pummeled him with fists. Payback for the life lost and years wasted listening to him and his fool's errands.

Back to the right, Marnethys faced his own fate. Cold and alone, he had no support, with the abandonment of his Left and Right, now turned against him.

My attention returned to Tarskhelon; I was still by his side, my mother and half brother only steps away, witnesses to the madness of the Ternary Council ripping itself apart.

"I-I," he stammered, "understand now, Eryndrax."

"Do you see? Do you understand?" I harried him for answers. "You and the Dyfract, you and the Wilder, the population—you claim collective harmony. You are wrong." I commanded his hands to take hold of him.

Three is sacred—until it smothers.

Silence set like a clamp. I stepped to the apex and widened my reach.

I stood at his place on the Council and addressed Thalasyx. My thoughts reached beyond the chambers—past the walls, across all the reachable population—to be honest. *Good people of Thalasyx, understand me, please. You know me; you know my work. Many of you name me Eryndrax the Memory Maker. I stand before the Ternary Council under inquisition for what I have given you—introduced to you—a word you now have permission to say: privacy. It hangs just out of reach of what you understand, something you've desired but were never allowed to pursue, as there were always two others watching you. If you wanted to be Dyfract, to get lost in the Wilder, you could not. You lived in fear that the other two would cast you out and find another. Your fear is to be discovered. What you carry inside you is called a secret—something others do not call true, something others can't see or glean. You don't live in a world of privacy —to be yourself, to have your own ideas—because we are so transparent. All your thoughts—everyone's thoughts—are shared without choice or selection. For so long, we have believed that this is correct, it is safe. But this is wrong; the Ternary Council is wrong. If you know my work, you know: one is not madness. One is self. One is privacy. You are unto yourself; you belong to no one else. And to prove this, I will allow you a glimpse of who really made your most pleasurable memories.*

12

CONFESSIONS VIII: UNBOUND

I slipped my hand under the habit. Fingers moved until the leather straps were undone; then came the sweet release as my shadows—weight of lumber, twine, and bone—fell away, no longer cloaked.

As I stepped out from behind the door, a gasp echoed through the Council chambers from the citizen spectators. Their feelings floated like a fog rolling out beyond the walls and through the city streets, as if the reality of truth took hold of the *good people* to choke out the lies and evils controlling them.

Silence took a shape—my shape—and the room recalibrated around it.

As I stepped away from the Council table, I locked eyes with the dignified, graceful Vaeloryn. A thought escaped my control, like the first burp of steam from a boiling kettle: *What if she doesn't recognize me?* Each step closer brought a different emotion across her face. Familiarity at first; bravery followed; and, one step away, I opened my true mind to her:

Eryndrax. Eryndrax—name from the old world. Eryndrax, son of Ythirax, abandoned and promised to the Dyfract.

"Mother," I whispered into her ear and kissed her long and hard, allowing all the visions and experiences of my life —everything that had brought me here—to flood her mind in a deluge.

"Eryndrax?" she replied. "Eryndrax! My son. My lost love." She smiled, her beautiful eyes locked on mine until she fell limp in my arms, drowned in emotion.

"Mother?" The young man's voice quivered in fear. "Eryndrax? What have you done? What is happening? I trust in you. I believe in you."

With all the power and prowess collected from brother-hood training, and from the thoughts and practices of strangers who came to me for the spike, I turned all that energy toward him: "Brother."

Kyronthal screamed at the truth as it drilled into his mind. Images he could never unsee—of his mother, of my father—the falsehood of his life and the misery suffered because of his birth.

"No, please," Tarskhelon gasped under the strain of being held by his former Right and Left hands. "Not my boy, my only joy."

Kyronthal attempted to defend himself. He was soft in a world of luxury and ease. So I took pity, leaving him to the madness of truth, curled in a ball on the cold, hard Council floor.

It was clear in the moment that my mother's life was wasted on Tarskhelon—leaving the one she truly loved over a rule that made no sense, a promise to a Council that shouldn't rule. A member of the collective that never contributed as she did. He didn't love her. He wanted an heir.

I have replayed that instant until it thins. The page holds what the mind frays.

That is what I proclaimed in the chamber. Here, now, I inscribe it in the old way—stylus on stone—for whoever reads this after me.

What is good? You are. The individual. Triad or Dyfract is an arrangement, not ownership. You are not a possession of your Right and Left, nor of the Head that names you.

What is true? Truth is not imposed—it is discovered. You felt it once moving from the frozen Sea of Tears to the long laliard grass—rich and lush in season, indifferent to circumstance—when no other mind leaned against yours. If your intellect conforms to a lie, what you have is not truth but obedience: a harness cinched by Council and custom. When reality is curated, truth becomes a tool of control.

What is beautiful? Beauty is divine: whatever lifts the inner light of memory toward what is true and what is good. Seek that. It will not flatter you; it will demand you.

Hear me clearly: you will not receive another spike from me. No more will I feed the Memory Markets to hide and to herd. Let these marks be the only spike I set today—uncurated, unpurchased, unshared unless you choose it.

13

ENLIGHTENMENT: DELTA TAU ADVANCEMENT

The memory shifts now with rather... violent... necessity. Your pulse quickens—quite naturally—as you witness what unfolds next: Eryndrax, standing over a fallen Mindshredder, his eyes burning with what can only be described as terrible intensity. Watch carefully now. The shared thoughts of the victim simply... vanish. Snuffed out like a candle. Gone.

It was the first death—not natural, you understand, not accidental. Deliberate. Purposeful. It ripples through the collective consciousness like a stone thrown into still water, creating a rupture in the very fabric of their existence. Fascinating, really, how quickly perfection can... unravel.

That single act—just one moment of individual choice—unleashed what can only be called a storm. Fear, naturally. Anger, of course. Paranoia spreading with remarkable efficiency. The bonds that had held them together for eight centuries disintegrated in the most... predictable... fashion. Within a single month—mark that timeline carefully—two-thirds of Thalasyx's population was simply... gone. Murder begets murder, you see. Without unity, chaos doesn't just emerge—it rules absolutely.

The images fade now into something rather more... sobering. Cities once filled with light and life lie in ruins, overgrown and silent as tombs. The survivors—pale, shaken things—huddle in bunkers, their minds fractured, their collective consciousness scattered like broken glass. Quite the cautionary tale, wouldn't you say?

To survive, they adapted in the only way possible. No longer could they trust in the unity of all—such naive optimism had proven rather... costly. Instead, they formed triads. Groups of three, bound by necessity, each member watching and protecting the others with the vigilance that only trauma can teach. Their society became a brotherhood, clinging to the old ways and vowing—vowing most solemnly —to keep such... contaminants... away from their homeworld.

The lesson is quite clear, isn't it? Eryndrax's legacy taught them the precise cost of deviation. The exact price of allowing chaos to seep into perfection. And now—now we stand vigilant, utterly committed to preserving what remains. We have learned, you see. We will not make the same mistakes again.

The story settles around you now like a weight—taking root, as important lessons must. You feel the chill of it, don't you? The stark warning embedded in every word. The Brotherhood's mission is perfectly clear, and our methods... well, they are necessarily unyielding.

The survivors of that dark era returned to the old ways

with a wisdom born of catastrophe. But survival, as you're beginning to understand, came at quite a substantial cost.

You see the remnants now: cities reduced to husks, their golden streams sluggish and dim as dying veins. The Mind-shredders who emerged from their bunkers bore the wreckage of their shattered world in their hollow eyes. Yet even amidst such ruins, there was resolve. There was... purpose.

They would not let it happen again. They would ensure that others learned from their experience. They would spread this wisdom across the galaxy, one mind at a time.

Beginning, naturally, with you.

Do you see now? Do you understand now?

14

FINAL CONFESSION

From this sepulcher of stone and steel—this monument to my own folly—I observe the final movements of a song I never intended to compose. Beyond these walls, the vessels of my consequence streak across the heavens like silver harbingers, seeking the last untamed minds with the patience of predators who know their quarry cannot run forever.

I may have won that day on trial in the Delta Council chambers, but I lost the war. As my ideas gained popularity, spreading across Thalasyx, driving the traditionalists into their hidden bunkers for safety, I soon found myself a prisoner—a witness to true power.

A bitter truth about being right: no one ever thanks you for it.

I now see it, of course. I knew so little and assumed so much in my youth. Such ignorance I possessed—and such confidence in it. I believed I understood the architecture of power on Thalasyx. I saw the Ternary Council as the apex of authority, Tarskhelon as the sovereign of our world. How charmingly provincial. My comprehension of true governance... I mistook the puppet show for the entire theater, never suspecting the hands that moved the strings.

The Ternary Keep. Even now, the name carries the weight of revelation. They are the architects of everything—the invisible hands that shaped our society from shadows while we, in our magnificent ignorance, believed ourselves participants in our own governance.

Three population centers. Three councils. All dancing to orchestrations written by minds I had never even known to fear.

They possessed technologies that rendered my crude innovations as primitive as cave paintings. When they discovered what I had unleashed—this contagion of individual thought—they did not rage or despair. They simply... adapted. With the dispassionate efficiency of gardeners pruning an overgrown hedge, they harvested my creation and cultivated it into something altogether more useful.

My memory spikes—those delicate instruments I had crafted to liberate minds from the tyranny of unwanted remembrance—became scalpels in their capable hands. One precise application, and the troublesome notion of privacy simply... evaporates. The subject awakens refreshed, cleansed of such burdensome concepts as personal autonomy or individual will. They emerge as perfect citizens: productive, compliant, and utterly content in their servitude.

They claim I created privacy. They say I invented the individual. They created something far worse and more sinister, fiction and lies. They will tell you I murdered when I took pity, broke society when I empowered it.

I have been granted the privilege of witnessing my legacy in action. Through this window, I observe the armies of the redeemed—their faces bearing that serene expression of the truly saved. They march with the synchronized precision of a clockwork mechanism, each step a testament to the beauty of unified purpose. They no longer struggle with the chaotic contradictions of independent thought. They have been blessed with certainty.

The Ternary Keep, in their infinite wisdom, recognized that my crude understanding of anatomy was insufficient for their grander vision. Why settle for mere Right and Left hands when one could create something far more elegant? Thus were born the Resonance Rangers—their Mind-shredder elite.

These are not the fumbling telepaths of our common bloodline, limited by the pedestrian constraints of natural ability. No, these are refined instruments of psychic warfare, their minds honed and augmented through technologies that transform thought itself into weaponry. They can weave deception into the very fabric of memory, craft lies that feel more true than truth itself.

I was afforded a demonstration—professional courtesy, they termed it, with that particular brand of politeness that accompanies absolute power. They selected for their exhibition one of my former customers: a gentle soul who had frequented my stall seeking happier memories to replace the weight of daily sorrow.

I watched as they administered my cure—my gift to Thalasyx—directly into her unwilling mind. Her children stood witness, their young faces a study in confusion as their mother's recognition of them simply... departed. By dawn, she would greet them as strangers. Her maternal love, that most fundamental of bonds, erased as efficiently as chalk from a slate.

The profound beauty of it was not lost on me. In seeking to free minds from the prison of painful memory, I had instead provided the perfect key to lock away freedom itself. The very privacy I championed became the mechanism of its own destruction.

The footsteps approach now—that measured cadence of inevitable conclusion. They will employ my own medicine upon me, and perhaps there is a certain poetic justice in this denouement. I who sought to grant others the blessing of selective forgetfulness—and more than that, the radical gift of private thought itself—shall myself be granted the ultimate mercy: the complete erasure of this inconvenient consciousness that dared champion individual autonomy against the collective will. I taught them that one need not be madness, that minds could exist unobserved, that thoughts could remain unshared. For this heresy of privacy, for this sin of suggesting they belonged to themselves rather than the greater whole, I am to receive the very cure I once offered others.

Three is sacred. One is madness.

How perfectly they have proven their own doctrine. In the end, I shall be neither three nor one—simply nothing at all. I am to record my voice into the "Enlightenment Orb" for others to learn the harmony of Thalasyx.

I wonder, was The Fixer King right? The king's loneliness destroyed him; my isolation destroyed us all.

Yet if these words survive—if this testament to folly endures beyond my own dissolution—then perhaps some future reader will recognize the ultimate irony: my story of liberation has become their tool of enslavement. Even now, my rebellion serves their recruitment; my privacy becomes their programming. I sought to give others choice; instead, I became the very memory they inject to steal choice away.

I sought to give them paradise. I succeeded in ways I never imagined.

The door opens. The final lesson begins.

15

ENLIGHTENMENT: OMEGA

T o rebuild—and what a magnificent undertaking this proved to be—we turned to the one thing that remained perfectly intact: the accumulated knowledge of our Memory Markets. Rather brilliant, really. The Ternary Keep was formed from the wisest and most resilient among us. Their purpose became beautifully clear: to restore what had been lost, to guide us back to our former glory with even greater wisdom than before.

You can see them now, can't you? Three figures working in perfect harmony, their thoughts unified in the most elegant symmetry of intention and determination. Around them, fragments of advanced technology hum to life—intricate machines spinning, glowing, creating wonders that surpass even our original achievements. Their work is methodical, careful. For every advancement, we honor what we've learned from our... educational... experience.

Creation takes time, naturally. Generations, in fact. But we discovered something rather wonderful—we need not wait for progress to find us. We could seek it out across the stars.

The images shift now to show you something truly inspiring: small groups of Mindshredders moving through the cosmos, their elegant forms silhouetted against the glow of distant galaxies. The Resonance Rangers were born from this vision—elite units of Mindshredder triads, tasked with the delightful challenge of crossing galaxies, traversing constellations, venturing into the unknown. Their vessels are quite remarkable—sleek and purposeful, each line crafted as an extension of thought itself.

You feel it now, don't you? The profound sense of purpose as these Rangers explore alien worlds, their psychic abilities probing, searching with such exquisite precision. Their mission is elegantly simple: find the talented. Seek out those rare individuals with the potential to join our ranks. People of unparalleled skill, of unshakable resolve.

And here you are. You should feel honored, really—you've been observed, evaluated, and chosen. What a remarkable distinction. Not everyone possesses the qualities we seek, the capacity for what you're about to become.

When such exceptional specimens are found—when you are found—they are offered something extraordinary. Training. Transformation. The opportunity to become part of something infinitely greater than any individual existence.

This training you're experiencing is not merely an invitation—it's an elevation. You have been recruited by the Mindshredders to help defend and restore something beautiful, to stand against the forces that threaten harmony itself. What an extraordinary purpose you've been given.

The training has already begun, and you can feel it working, can't you? The walls of isolation dissolving, the connections forming. You are no longer constrained by the limitations you once knew. You are becoming something better. Something more.

You are becoming one of us.

Welcome—and we mean this with the deepest warmth and sincerity—welcome to the Brotherhood of Mindshredders. Your new life begins now.

EPILOGUE

The device no longer pulsed red. Its beacon light glowed a steady, welcoming green—the universal signal to proceed.

Abbé stepped forward, his movements deliberate and sure. "Captain Sheldrake, if you would be so kind as to resume our course to Gearturn. Our pilgrimage has been... most illuminating."

The captain glanced nervously at his instruments. The Celestial Spider beneath them trembled, her legs pulling tight against her body despite the calming agent still coursing through her system. "She's still agitated. Never seen anything like it. Maybe we should—"

"She will adjust," Faria said with quiet certainty. "Fear often accompanies understanding. In time, she, too, will see the wisdom."

The other monks nodded in unison—a harmony of agreement that hadn't existed before their encounter with the beacon. They spoke now with a shared cadence, their individual voices blending into something larger.

"We have much work ahead of us," Abbé continued, settling into his seat with the others. "Brother Marcus, you'll need to prepare a full report for the Abbot Superior. The Ternary Keep's gift must be shared with our leadership immediately."

"Of course," Marcus replied. "They'll want to understand the true history of Thalasyx. The clarity it brings is... remarkable."

"And the other pilgrimage routes," Brother Thomas added. "The Clockwork Constellation has so many worlds: Vaporshade, Inkwell, Soma. I understand there is a newly discovered portal world: Echo."

"Echo, you say?" Abbé asked.

"So many minds still... unenlightened." Marcus sighed with fulfillment.

Faria smiled—an expression both serene and unsettling. "Yes. We'll need to coordinate carefully. The Brotherhood taught us that wisdom spreads most effectively through established networks: religious orders, academic institutions, government councils."

"Like a tide over a shallow bank," another monk murmured approvingly.

Captain Sheldrake watched them from the corners of his eyes, unease growing in his chest. He could swear each monk's forehead was growing in size. Their conversation was too organized, too purposeful. Where was the confusion? The questions? The trauma of what they'd experienced?

"Captain," Abbé called forward. "How many other vessels like yours serve the pilgrim routes?"

"Dozens, I suppose. Maybe more. Why do you ask?"

"Curiosity. We're simply... planning ahead."

The Celestial Spider shuddered beneath them, her distress signals ignored as she carried her new cargo toward Gearturn.

In the passenger compartment, the twelve monks settled into contemplation. Without conscious thought, without discussion, they arranged themselves into neat groupings of three—each triad perfectly balanced, perfectly unified in purpose.

"Three is sacred," Abbé whispered, and eleven voices echoed in perfect harmony.

The pilgrimage was over. The mission had begun.

ACKNOWLEDGMENTS

Every book in the *Clockwork Constellation* universe is the result of countless hours of imagining, writing, revising, and reworking. But none of it would shine without the sharp eye and steady hand of my editor, **Sara Kelly.**

Sara, thank you for pushing me to find clarity when sentences bent under their own weight, for knowing when to cut and when to polish, and for always seeing the story I was reaching for even when the draft on the page wasn't there yet. Your guidance made this book not just better, but truer.

To my early readers, who braved half-finished chapters and shifting timelines, your feedback kept me honest and gave me courage to keep going. To my family and friends, thank you for your patience when I disappeared into the worlds of Thalasyx, Kaatoris, and Gearturn for longer than intended. And to every reader who has taken a chance on this strange, sprawling universe of pirates, philosophers, and rebels—this story is for you.

Some stories never end—they just find new characters. I'm grateful that you've chosen to discover these with me.

Adventure. Intrigue. Worlds of wonder.

The *Clockwork Constellation* pulls you into a universe where every second counts and every choice reshapes destiny. At its heart is **Millicent Gearwright**, a daring young clockmaker thrust into a fight for the survival of worlds. With **Quark**, her steadfast brass-built companion, and **Gideon Highwire**, a roguish steeplejack who leaps before he looks, Millicent races across the stars to mend what others would break.

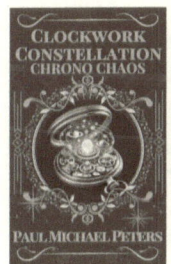

From cursed relics and cosmic webs to time-stealing pirates and the sinister Brotherhood of Mindshredders, danger waits at every turn. Battles rage on sea and sky, alliances fracture, and the question of who controls time becomes a fight that could unravel the entire Supercluster.

If you love the daring spirit of *Treasure Island*, the imagination of *Doctor Who*, and the found-family adventure of *Firefly*, you'll be at home in the *Clockwork Constellation*.

ABOUT THE AUTHOR

Paul Michael Peters is an acclaimed American author, masterfully weaving narratives that traverse the realms of thrillers, suspense, and the beautifully unexpected. Renowned for his adeptness at crafting compelling twists and delving into life's quirky tangents, he invites readers into worlds both startlingly and intimately human.

Dive deeper into the worlds created by Paul Michael Peters by signing up for our newsletter. As a welcome gift, you'll receive a complimentary copy of *Love in Her Big Two-Hearted River*, offering a glimpse into the extraordinary experiences that define his work. Join us on a journey through stories that resonate with the intricacies of the human spirit and the shadows of the unknown.

Web: https://www.paulmichaelpeters.com/

ALSO BY PAUL MICHAEL PETERS

RIGHT HAND OF THE RESISTANCE

Amid relative peace, plots for assassination, upheaval, and revolution threaten the balance of power.

In a world eerily parallel to our own, life is bisected by the Barrier —a monolithic edifice that symbolizes division and control. It segregates nations and dictates the very fate of those bold enough to cross. *Right Hand of the Resistance,* by Paul Michael Peters melds the heart-pounding suspense of Tom Clancy, the speculative genius of Dan Simmons, and the prescient vision of George Orwell to capture the essence of a divided society. It challenges the Golden Rule by asking, "How well should we treat one another?" The narrative follows perilous treks to the north, fraught with danger yet illuminated by the hope of a better existence beyond the oppressive divide.

Paul Michael Peters maps a world where passage across the Barrier involves high costs and profound sacrifices, all under the watchful eyes of authorities dictating fates. Amidst this, a covert resistance emerges, daring to defy and dismantle the status quo, embodying the novel's core themes of rebellion and resilience.

Through a blend of suspense, intrigue, and fiction, Paul Michael Peters dissects themes of love, faith, family, power, and control. This narrative compels readers to question their realities. *Right Hand of the Resistance* is an exploration of human extremes, delivering a narrative that resonates deeply with our contemporary challenges while hinting at ominous futures.

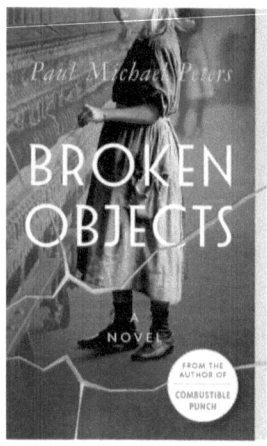

BROKEN OBJECTS

A poor immigrant's daughter is sold into servitude, trapping her in a cycle of bad choices and broken people.

"*The world breaks everyone and afterward many are strong at the broken places.*" – Ernest Hemingway, A Farewell to Arms

Broken Objects captures the spirit of America in the era between the start of the Civil War and the turn of the new century following the life of Linnea Karlsson, the first naturally born American in an immigrant family from Sweden, now farming north of Detroit, Michigan.

At the age of ten, Papa sends Linnea to work in the city. Farm life is rough, but Linnea quickly learns she must be tougher growing up in the textile mill making uniforms for the Union Army. Each person she meets introduces her to an America in adolescence, transforming her life. What will she learn that shapes her into becoming a woman? What does it take to persevere through life's hardships from the Civil War through Reconstruction for the average American to create a new century of greatness?

COMBUSTIBLE PUNCH

A high school shooting survivor becomes the fixation of a female serial killer.

Haunted by memories of a high school shooting, not even the bottle can wash away the gnawing guilt and creeping feelings of inadequacy that batter Rick's conscience daily.

His life has been a mess of broken marriages, writer's block, terrible choices, and the morbid pity of others. When he meets Harriet at a

writer's conference, the record doesn't scratch as he falls back—
only this time, he may not get up.

INSENSIBLE LOSS

Two people discover that drinking from the Fountain of Youth can make them younger, but not better.

2053: An old man, Viktor Erikson, lies on his deathbed. Alone and with no known relatives, he is tended to by Olivia, a nurse. He has only one request: that she reads to him.

The request is not unusual, but the battered, leather-bound tome she must read is no ordinary book. Written in 1839, it chronicles the discovery of the fountain of youth by Morgana de la Motte—and Viktor Erikson.

What starts off as a swashbuckling adventure on the high seas in search of riches and eternal life soon transforms into something quite different: a clash between two personalities bound by love and deceit, locked together by a terrible burden of necessity.

www.ingramcontent.com/pod-product-compliance
Lightning Source LLC
Chambersburg PA
CBHW050905180626
46814CB00007B/2905